Level 2 is idea
some reading inst
simple sentences

Special features:

Frequent repetition of main story words and phrases

Short, simple sentences

It was Jack's first day at pirate school.

Time to go!

6

7

Large, clear type

Careful match between story and pictures

There was the Pirate School ship. All aboard!

"Come on, Jack!" said Miss Crossbones. "All aboard the Pirate School ship."

Pirate School

WELCOME PIRATES

9

Kiara Lam
(21)
10

Educational Consultant: Geraldine Taylor
Book Banding Consultant: Kate Ruttle

A catalogue record for this book is available from the British Library

Published by Ladybird Books Ltd
80 Strand, London, WC2R 0RL
A Penguin Company

006
© LADYBIRD BOOKS LTD MMXIII
Ladybird, Read It Yourself and the Ladybird Logo are registered or
unregistered trademarks of Ladybird Books Limited.

ISBN: 978-0-71819-469-7

Printed in China

Pirate School

Written by Mandy Ross
Illustrated by Kim Geyer

It was Jack's first day
at pirate school.

Time to go!

7

There was the Pirate
School ship. All aboard!

"Come on, Jack!" said
Miss Crossbones.
"All aboard the Pirate
School ship."

"It's time for the first lesson," said Miss Crossbones. "Come and read the treasure map." They all read the treasure map.

"Tip-top! Now it's time for the next lesson," said Miss Crossbones. "How to rescue a pirate."

Jack rescued Ella. Then Ella rescued Jack.

"Tip-top! Now it's time for the next lesson," said Miss Crossbones. "How pirates sail a ship. First, the ship's anchor is pulled up."

They all pulled up the ship's anchor. Then they sailed out to sea, past Shark Waters and Danger Deeps.

"Look!" said Jack.
"It's Pirate Island!"

"Put down the ship's anchor," said Miss Crossbones. "Now, all look for the treasure!"

"Where will it be?" said Jack

They looked here. They looked there. They looked all over the island.

At last, Jack said, "Here's the treasure! It was down a deep hole, just like on the map."

All aboard! They pulled up the ship's anchor and sailed back out to sea.

Pirate School

19

"Where is Miss Crossbones?" said Ella. "Is she back on Pirate Island?"

They sailed all the way back, past Shark Waters and Danger Deeps.

Danger Deeps

Shark Waters

21

The pirates looked here. They looked there. They looked all over the island.

22

23

"Help! Help!" said Miss Crossbones.

"Look!" said Jack. "She is down this deep hole! We will rescue you, Miss Crossbones!"

They all rescued Miss Crossbones, just like the lesson.

"Tip-top!" said Miss Crossbones. "Now, all aboard the ship!"

The pirates sailed all the way back, past Danger Deeps and Shark Waters... just in time!

"A tip-top first day at Pirate School!" said Miss Crossbones.

29

How much do you remember about the story of Pirate School? Answer these questions and find out!

- Where does Jack go to school?

- What is the name of his teacher?

- Which two places do the pirates sail past?

- Where do they find the treasure?